DAYENU DAYENU

four collections of "Dayenu"
cartoons in a single volume

by HENRY LEONARD

ABOUT COMICS, CAMARILLO, CALIFORNIA

All "publisher's notes" are from the publisher of the original editions:
Crown Publishers, New York.

About Comics thanks Mordechai Luchins for
bringing this work to our attention

ISBN-13: 978-1-949996-49-4

Continuous printing starting September, 2022

Address all inquiries, including wholesale and customized edition orders, to
questions@aboutcomics.com

OPEN YOUR MOUTH AND SAY "OY"

"A Special Kind of Saltiness"

The cartoons in this book were selected from the Dayenu (Da-yay-noo) series which has won a unique reputation in the world of humor. The first of these appeared several years ago in the Los Angeles *Jewish Voice*. They were extraordinarily funny, they were *new*, they had a wry, gentle-spoof quality, and soon the Dayenu cartoons were appearing in English-language Jewish publications all over the country, in Canada, England, Scotland, Australia and South Africa.

The name "Dayenu" derives from one of the most popular and best known prayers in the Jewish litany. Freely translated, it means "We'd be satisfied," or "It would have been enough for us," or simply "Accepted." It is the response of the congregation when the reader recites, "If the Lord had brought us out of Egypt but had not made a path in the Red Sea for us"—"Dayenu," "If the Lord had made a path in the Red Sea for us but had not blown down the walls of Jericho"—"Dayenu," and so on. It is typical of a Jewish attitude—to savor whatever goodness has been granted, to look for the bright side always and somehow to find it.

It should be mentioned that Henry Leonard is a pseudonym for a team. Henry Rabin, Director of the B'nai Brith Hillel Foundation at Los Angeles City and State Colleges, conceives the cartoon ideas. The man who actually draws the cartoons is Leonard Pritikin, who by profession is an advertising and art director.

Jewish humor has a special kind of saltiness, and in these

cartoons Henry Leonard displays the fine flavor of Jewish wit at its best. Despite the fact that most of them deal with various facets of American-Jewish life, they are nonetheless truly universal in their appeal. They amuse and delight non-Jews as well as Jews and so they deserve wider and more general publication. We feel fortunate that we were able to arrange for the publication of this book.

The Publishers

DAYENU HAS APPEARED IN THE FOLLOWING ANGLO-JEWISH
PUBLICATIONS TO WHOM ACKNOWLEDGMENTS ARE
GRATEFULLY MADE

Atlanta, Ga.	*The Southern Israelite*
Atlantic City, N. J.	*The Jewish Record*
Baltimore, Md.	*The Baltimore Jewish Times*
Birmingham, Ala.	*The Jewish Monitor*
Boston, Mass.	*The Jewish Advocate*
Buffalo, N. Y.	*The Buffalo Jewish Review*
Camden, N. J.	*The Voice*
Cape Town, So. Africa	*The South African Jewish Chronicle*
Chicago, Ill.	*The Sentinel*
Cincinnati, Ohio	*Every Friday*
Cleveland, Ohio	*The Jewish Review and Observer*
Columbus, Ohio	*The Ohio Jewish Chronicle*
Denver, Colo.	*The Intermountain Jewish News*
Detroit, Mich.	*The Detroit Jewish News*
Douglaston, N. Y.	*The Scroll*
Fresno, Cal.	*Central Valley Jewish Heritage*
Glasgow, Scotland	*The Jewish Echo*
Indianapolis, Ind.	*The Indiana Jewish Chronicle*
Jacksonville, Fla.	*The Southern Jewish Weekly*
Jersey City, N. J.	*The Jewish Standard*
Johannesburg, South Africa	*The Zionist Record*
Long Island, N. Y.	*The Long Island Jewish Press*
Los Angeles, Calif.	*The Jewish Voice*
Manchester, England	*The Jewish Telegraph*
Memphis, Tenn.	*The Hebrew Watchman*
Miami, Fla.	*The Jewish Floridian*

7

Minneapolis, Minn.	*The American Jewish World*
Montreal, Canada	*The Canadian Jewish Chronicle*
Nashville, Tenn.	*The Observer*
New York, N. Y.	*The American Examiner*
Phoenix, Ariz.	*Phoenix Jewish News*
Pittsburgh, Pa.	*The American Jewish Outlook*
San Antonio, Tex.	*The B'nai B'rith Voice*
San Diego, Calif.	*The Southwest Jewish Press*
San Francisco, Calif.	*The Jewish Community Bulletin*
South Bend, Ind.	*Our Community*
Springfield, Mass.	*Jewish Weekly News*
St. Paul, Minn.	*St. Paul Jewish News*
St. Petersburg, Fla.	*The Suncoast Jewish News*
Sydney, Australia	*The Sydney Jewish News*
Toronto, Canada	*The Daily Hebrew Journal*
Tucson, Ariz.	*The Arizona Post*
Vancouver, Canada	*The Jewish Western Bulletin*
Washington, D. C.	*The Jewish Digest*
Washington, D. C.	*The B'nai B'rith Women's World*
Waterbury, Conn.	*Jewish Community Bulletin*
Westchester, N. Y.	*Westchester Jewish Tribune*
Winnipeg, Canada	*The Jewish Post*
Worcester, Mass.	*The Jewish Civic Leader*

"Now, Bobe, open your mouth and say <u>Oy</u>."

"Polly wanta matzos!"

"Nonsense . . . Your son can learn Hebrew
with just this one easy record . . ."

"And don't forget, the Hebrew records you play BACKWARDS."

"It wasn't at all like The Book."

"Before our Torah reading let us bid a hearty 'Shalom Aleichem' to our good friends who must now leave on Inter-American Airlines Flight 73."

"Well, at least Grandpa digs my beatnik
friends. He thinks they're Yeshiva students."

"In our temple, Rabbi, you may speak on
any subject . . . as long as it isn't controversial."

"Rabbi, down heah we don't mind you preachin'
against social injustice . . . as long as you all
don't get too specific."

"Oh, by the way, dear . . . the Rabbi's coming
to dinner tonight."

"QUICK . . . ZEDE'S COMING!"

"Mr. Goldstein, must you answer all my questions with a question?"

"All right . . . who's the noodnik that's putting **PIGS** in the animal crackers?"

"Athiest schmeithiest! You're still going to shul."

"No, David, the person who visits all Jewish homes at this time on Passover night is Elijah . . . NOT Superman!"

"And today I am a MAN!"

It's hard to be a Jew.

The bread of affliction . . . ?

"It's our most popular model. When the Rabbi speaks longer than one hour, it automatically collapses."

"Why, we wouldn't think of changing your name, my dear. **YETTA GINSBERG** will be sensational at the box office!"

"All right, Rabbi, I'll give another $250,000 for the New Temple Building Fund, but only on condition that you treat me just like any other member."

"Who said you HAVE to be a doctor or lawyer?
If you want to be a plumber it's perfectly all
right with us . . ."

"What, so few present again? Always a
full house for our religious services and
nobody for our socials!"

"Our Rabbi's sermons are so short. I do wish he'd speak longer."

"This year, gentlemen, all teachers have been instructed
to place the emphasis mainly on Chanukah."

"Must you always go out with rich boys . . . can't you date a poor boy once in a while?"

"Davy, believe me . . . any girl that's good
enough for YOU to marry is good enough
for me."

"Today I am not a Man, but a scared Bar-Mitzvah kid who knows from nothing about Judaism."

"Didn't the grown-ups ever do anything?"

"At school the teacher said that we Jews are the 'Children of the Book'. . . What book does she mean, Pa?"

"BOY! Did he break that glass!"

"Becky, he says we should be in
Nairobi for Shabbas."

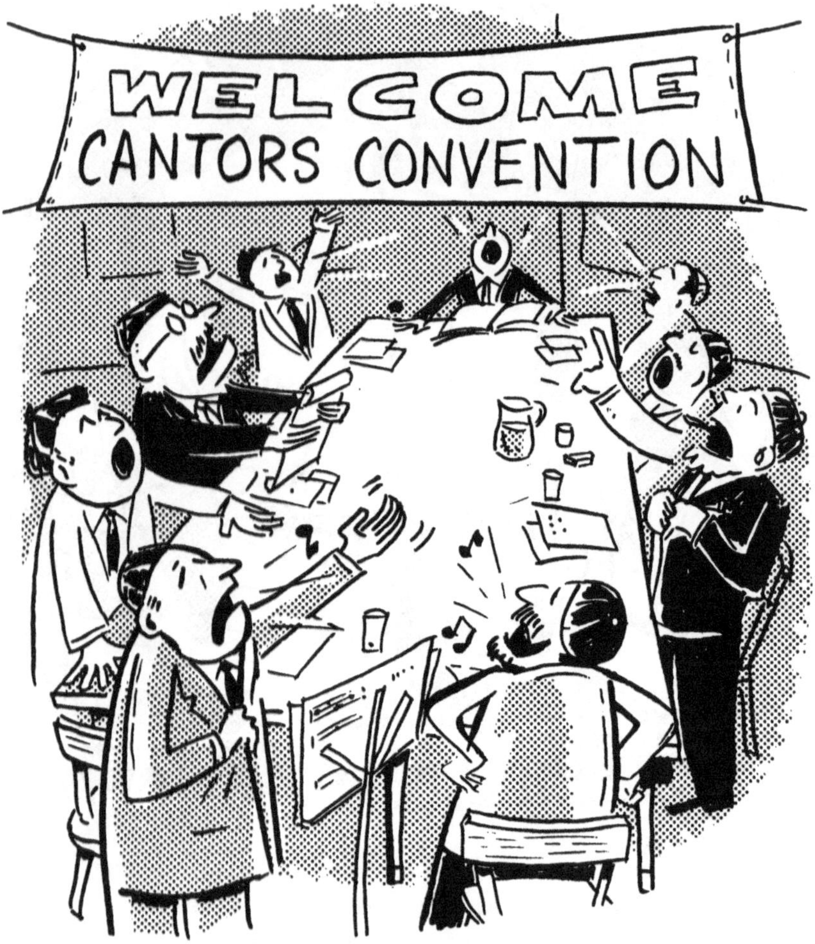
WELCOME
CANTORS CONVENTION

"After a two years' absence, Mr. Levine, it's a real pleasure seeing you in shul this Shabbas morning. Are you running for councilman again?

"My shofar is bigger
than your shofar."

". . . and next time, Mr. Goldstein,
don't call me 'shammas'!"

"So you're studying for the rabbinate, eh? Wha.
kind of business is THAT for a good Jewish boy?"

"Sorry, Ma'm. Ah don't hanker for no kreplach tonight."

"And if you wish to hear Cantor Blackstein sing grace after your meal, just press button number 16 on the jukebox."

"And so, children, our princess met a nice Jewish boy, got married and lived happily ever after."

"Mrs. Klein, let's put it this way. You have two personalities . . . a **KOSHER** one and a **TREFE**."

"And for making this Bar-Mitzvah day possible, I should like to thank my dear parents, my sister and brother, my beloved Hebrew teacher, Mr. Boyarsky, and my devoted psychiatrist, Dr. MacDonald."

"Epstein's from Texas."

"Father, wherefore is this night different from all
other nights . . . and you may have 20 seconds in
which to answer."

"And next week our Regular Friday Night Services will be at 5:30 P.M., our Late Services at 8 P.M., and our Late-Late Services at 9:30."

"Look, Hannah, how my son Max loves me.
He writes that he goes every day to a doctor
with a couch, and spends a whole hour just
talking about me."

"How can I go to sleep, Molly, when I know my
competitor, Beryl, is awake scheming . . . ?"

"Mr. Speaker, with over **400** eruptions against Houses
of Worship, schools and homes in the last two years,
the time for action has now come! Hence, I propose a
commission be set up at once for a long-range
study of the problem."

"Oh, Edna, please come in to interpret again.
Mrs. Shapiro only speaks Yiddish . . ."

Two sets of plates.

"My dear friends . . . we Jews must learn to get
closer to one another."

"It says, 'GIVE TO THE JUDAEAN
WELFARE FUND.' "

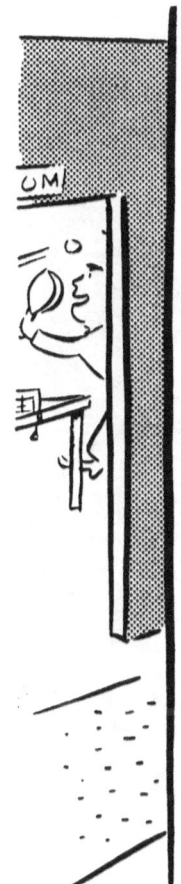

JEWISH CULTURAL CENTER

TUES. - PING PONG TOURNAMENT

THURS. - SQUARE DANCE

SUN. - LECTURE:
"HOW TO GET A MATE"

MON. - BASKET WEAVING

WED. - MOVIE NITE
MARILYN MONROE !!!!!!!!"

SAT. - SWIMMING CLASS

MON. - INDIAN BEAD STRINGING

"Fifth floor . . . Hebrew Cultural Society."

"Mom, we're out of TREFE again!"

"Yes, I did ask you to build a temple in keeping
with modern times, BUT . . ."

"Which shul do you belong to
. . . Channel 5 or Channel 9?"

NEVER ON SHABBAS!

FOREWORD

"Dayenu" ("It would have been sufficient for us") is the refrain of a song in the Passover service. The song enumerates the abundant favors which God conferred on Israel and concludes each blessing with the word, "Dayenu," implying that each favor was sufficient to obligate Israel to great thankfulness.

"Dayenu" is a serious term yet it lends itself very well to this particular aspect of our people—the ability to poke fun at ourselves. Even historian Renan, who was not particularly friendly to us, understood this very well; "If you write about Jews you will learn all about humor."

We are a people for whom everything is sacrosanct yet for whom nothing is sacred. Certainly nothing about American-Jewish life is sacred—for which we can only say, Dayenu. To take ourselves too seriously is to make life not only parochial but impossible.

And it is no coincidence that many of the great humorists of the Western world, both in literature and on the stage, have been Jews. The scholar Israel Knox gives us an important insight into this phenomenon, ("Jewish Heritage," February, 1962):

"One of the dominant elements (Jewish humor) was skepticism—the habit of doubt, the shrug of the shoulder . . . What better precaution (than humor) could there be in an environment without guarantees for (Jewish) stability . . ."

Jews understood, too, that nothing makes quicker communication between people than a good laugh. We have to laugh at ourselves because we own both a public and a private *self,* and only by laughing do both *selves* see and understand each other.

Never on Shabbas is a pretty concise analysis of our private *selves,* for which we ought to thank Rabbi Henry Rabin and Leonard Pritikin. If they had given us only the cartoon on page 1, we should have to say, "Dayenu."

Harry Golden

Charlotte, North Carolina
March 1, 1962

This, the second collection of Dayenu (Da-yay-noo) cartoons, follows the outstanding success of OPEN YOUR MOUTH AND SAY "OY." The cartoons are created by Henry Leonard, a name which represents a team. Henry Rabin, Director of the B'nai B'rith Hillel Foundations at Los Angeles City and State Colleges, originates the ideas; the man who actually draws the cartoons is Leonard Pritikin, professionally an advertising director.

Even though the humor, insight and irony are directed at situations in Jewish life, the appeal of Dayenu cartoons is so universal that they delight Jew and non-Jew alike. For readers unfamiliar with Jewish words and terms, we have included a glossary on the next page. As in the previous collection, the cartoons were selected from the series appearing in English-language Jewish publications in many countries throughout the world, to whom we gratefully acknowledge our thanks:

Atlanta, Ga.......*The Southern Israelite*
Atlantic City, N. J....*The Jewish Record*
Baltimore, Md..............*The Baltimore Jewish Times*
Birmingham, Ala....*The Jewish Monitor*
Boston, Mass. ......*The Jewish Advocate*
Buffalo, N. Y. ....*The Buffalo Jewish Review*
Camden, N. J. ....*The Voice*
Cape Town, So. Africa....... *The South African Jewish Chronicle*
Chicago, Ill. ....*The Sentinel*
Cincinnati, Ohio..............*Every Friday*
Cleveland, Ohio.......*The Jewish Review and Observer*
Columbus, Ohio.................... *The Ohio Jewish Chronicle*
Denver, Colo.........*The Intermountain Jewish News*
Des Moines, Iowa......*The News Letter*
Detroit, Mich....................*The Detroit Jewish News*
Douglaston, N. Y.................*The Scroll*
El Paso, Texas......... *Jewish Community Voice*
Fresno, Cal..................*Central Valley Jewish Heritage*

Galveston, Texas ....*The Bulletin*
Glasgow, Scotland.....*The Jewish Echo*
Indianapolis, Ind................*The Indiana Jewish Chronicle*
Jacksonville, Fla............ *The Southern Jewish Weekly*
Jersey City, N. J....*The Jewish Standard*
Johannesburg, South Africa *The Zionist Record*
Long Island, N. Y........*The Long Island Jewish Press*
Los Angeles, Calif......*The Jewish Voice*
Manchester, England...........*The Jewish Telegraph*
Melbourne, Australia............*Australian Jewish Herald*
Memphis, Tenn...............*The Hebrew Watchman*
Miami, Fla..........*The Jewish Floridian*
Minneapolis, Minn........*The American Jewish World*
Montreal, Canada...........*The Canadian Jewish Chronicle*
Nashville, Tenn...............*The Observer*
Newark, N. J. *American Jewish Ledger*
New York, N. Y.............*The American Examiner*
New York, N. Y...............*World Over*

GLOSSARY

BAR MITZVAH. Name for confirmed Jewish boy thirteen years old, or name of the ceremony itself.

CHANUKAH. Eight-day festival celebrated in December in honor of ancient Jewish struggle for religious freedom.

CHOMETZ. All leavened food prohibited during Passover.

GALITZEANERS. Jews from Galicia.

GEFILTE FISH. A form of stuffed fish.

GESUNT AUF DEINE KEPPELE. Yiddish expression meaning "May you be blessed."

KIDDUSH. A benediction offered over wine.

LITVAKS. Jews from Lithuania.

MACHER. An important person.

MATZOS. Unleavened bread.

MEZUZAH. A small case, containing Bible passages, found on doorposts of Jewish homes.

NOSHERAI. Sweets or goodies.

NU? Well? So what?

PASSOVER. An eight-day festival commemorating the Jewish deliverance from Egypt.

REBBE. Hebrew teacher or Rabbi.

ROSH HASHANAH. Jewish New Year.

SHABBAS. Sabbath or Saturday.

SHADCHAN. Marriage broker.

SHAMMAS. A Jewish sexton.

SHUL. A synagogue.

SUCCOTH. The Feast of Tabernacles.

SUKKAH. A roofless hut used during the Feast of Tabernacles.

TALLITH. A prayer shawl.

YARMALKE. Skull cap worn in synagogue.

YESHIVAH. An advanced Religious School of Jewish learning.

YOM KIPPUR. The day of atonement.

ZEDE. Grandfather.

"Every Yom Kippur the Rabbi always preaches about our greed and selfishness. Why doesn't he stick to religion?"

"But, Sir, my daughter already donated . . . in Sunday
School."

"Next time you'll listen when the Rebbe gives you
instructions."

"Rabbi, why does my daddy smoke in the bathroom on Shabbas, and eat there on Yom Kippur?"

Every Jew a Macher

"Ah . . . that's why Mendel is always late on his route. He kisses all the mezuzahs!"

"All right, go and say it . . . it's because we went
fishing on Shabbas."

"As we conclude this Yom Kippur day, I wish to inform our annual guests that our Rosh Hashanah Services will begin next year at 6:45 p.m."

"There goes Beryl, the weightlifter, showing off
again!"

"And next on our agenda will be a discussion on an appropriate blessing over Metrecal."

"I don't like to either, David, but we have to for our children's sake."

"Sorry Madam . . . but Chanukah preceded Christmas
this year."

"There goes Rabbi Nubkin with his Sukkah-Mobile."

"Rabbi, maybe you can help me. How can I stay away from shul and still not feel guilty about it?"

"And Sam, darling, for Passover, don't forget . . .
bring home a carton of matzos, matzo meal, chopped
nuts, and a big box of bicarb . . ."

"And for the New Year, Mrs. Epstein, there should be peace in the world, prosperity for everybody, freedom for all mankind, and a husband for my daughter, Ellie."

"Take me to your Rabbi."

"Officers of Temple Beth-El, members of the Temple Board, members of my family, mourners and any chance worshippers at this Friday night service . . ."

"Don't you think we should attend at least ONE
meeting?"

"It isn't at all like the movie."

"And after the Rabbi's sermon, to help reawaken the Congregation, we'll sing psalm number . . . "

"On this Bar Mitzvah day I can categorically state I am not a man, but rather a youngster emerging from puberty to advanced adolescence, and sharing with you the ambivalent emotions of which I am bounteously sensitized."

"Look, Noah, you save 'em in your way and I'll save 'em in mine."

"And so, folks, eight nights of Chanukah or not . . .
all I expect is just one present."

"You say you want a Chanukah present? A gesunt auf deine keppele!"

"Daddy, do Gentiles believe in Christmas, too?"

"And here, Mr. Nathan, is your Rabbi, whom you haven't seen since you joined his temple 15 years ago."

"Rabbi, since I prefer English, please use no Hebrew in the ceremony; since I'm not religious, no theology; and since I'm in a hurry . . . please omit the Sermon."

"But, Rabbi, my head IS covered."

"Lunar Expedition F42 calling Earth . . . Since one day
up here lasts two weeks, Corporal Hyman wants to
know what to do about Shabbas."

"Oh I always bring the baby to shul. The Rabbi's
sermon just works wonders."

"And next week our services will feature a Kiddush chanted by Cantor Blackstein in three dimensional stereo."

"Irving, when you leave, must you always kiss me like I'm a mezzuzah?"

"And don't forget, Mac, . . . for your lunch today in the garment district, it's a kosher corned beef sandwich on rye!"

"David, let's buy this plot . . . it's only five minutes
from the subway."

"The Stork Club or the Copa, Sam. It doesn't matter,
'For whither thou goest, I will go'."

"Nu, Doctor, stop crying already, so I can tell you
the rest of my troubles!"

"You can tell it's time for the High Holidays when
Beryl, the shammas, begins oiling the seats."

"And now that our Shabbas services are over, I should like to present and thank the members of our temple choir . . . Mr. Haggarty, Miss Johnson, Mrs. O'Conner and Mrs. Whitney."

"What do I think of my grandchildren? Oh, they're just average."

"Rabbi, this is my husband, David Rabinowitz, and my two sons, Jerry Robin and Bill Rayburn."

"That's Manny's new all-weather Sukkah. With that weather-eye, the umbrella opens automatically at the first raindrop."

"It says, 'Weight, 150 . . . and take it easy on the
nosherai.' "

"When you're ready, just press this button, then the
ark and pulpit will disappear and you'll have your
full-size basketball court."

"It's the only way Zede will go in."

"Doctor, it must be Yom Kippur time again . . . there are three cantors in the waiting room with laryngitis."

"Girls, now a speech by Rabbi Nubkin, then we'll get to the more important matters of the afternoon."

"My dear friends, before I speak this evening, I
would like to make a few remarks . . . "

130

"We interrupt our Shabbas Service to announce that at the end of the fifth inning, the Yankees are leading by . . . "

"Fred, for Passover why don't you get a new Tallith,
and I'LL get a new mink stole?"

"Let's ask the Chief Rabbi where the Mezuzah goes
on this revolving door."

"What did I tell you! In that part of Jersey, Litvaks
DO outnumber Galitzeaners two to one."

"And to think, Son, in my day we just used to call him 'The Shammas'."

"If Churchill and Eisenhower only listened to me years ago, Max, we'd never be in such a mess today."

"Hawkins, please show the Rebbe to Junior's room.
It's time for his Hebrew lesson."

"On our agenda tonight, gentlemen, we have two items: the falling plaster in the men's room, and the future of American Judaism."

"And I wanna give 500 bucks to the Red Cross, and 500 bucks to the Torah V'daas Fund of the 43rd Street Yeshivah."

"Nu, Sarah . . . so a little competition never hurt anyone."

"If you'll just be patient, sir, I'm sure we have a copy of the Bible somewhere."

"No, it's not a screen test. My cousin Moe is getting married."

"All right, Stern, I'll go to yours tonight, if you go to mine next week."

"Look at him . . . one day in the hospital and he's
already taking his own blood pressure!"

"And I propose, Mr. Chairman, that our answer to this anti-semitic act should be a **COURAGEOUS SILENCE!**"

"We begin our COMPLETE services on page 50. . . omit the Hebrew on pages 51 to 56 . . . then skip to the middle of page 64."

"If God helps, and is willing, and we are healthy, and all goes well, and we live . . . I'll see you tomorrow at two o'clock."

"She wants to know what time to light the Shabbas
Candles tonight."

WITH A LITTLE
BIT OF
MAZEL-TOV!

**"IT'S TRIPLETS, MR. ROTHSTEIN.
MAZEL-TOV! MAZEL-TOV! MAZEL-TOV!"**

ACKNOWLEDGMENT

The author would like to acknowledge the invaluable assistance of Rabbi William Kramer, of Los Angeles, whose incisive wit and creative mind have helped give birth to many a Dayenu cartoon. "Todah Rabah!"

Readers of OPEN YOUR MOUTH AND SAY OY and NEVER ON SHABBAS will recall that the cartoons in those books, as in this, were selected from the Dayenu (Da-yay-noo) series, unique in the world of humor. Because of the excellence of those cartoons and their wide appeal to Jewish audiences, they now appear in over 60 English-language Jewish publications in the United States, Canada, England, the Netherlands, Austria, and South Africa.

The wry, penetrating humor touches on all phases of American-Jewish life. Scarcely a reader cannot say of at least a dozen or more of the situations, "Why, this is just the way it happened to *me!*" The authors (Henry Leonard is really two: Rabbi Henry Rabin, Director of the B'nai B'rith Hillel Foundations at Los Angeles City College and San Fernando Valley State College, creates the cartoon ideas; Leonard Pritikin, advertising and art director, draws the cartoons) have managed to capture the foibles, inconsistencies and incongruities of Jewish life and present them in such universally appealing form that virtually everyone responds. So here is a wonderful collection of laughter-evoking Dayenu cartoons guaranteed to provide enjoyment for all who behold them.

The Publishers

The authors gratefully mention the following
Anglo-Jewish publications, in which these
"Dayenu" cartoons have appeared . . .

Boston, Mass.......*The Jewish Advocate*
Buffalo, N. Y...*Buffalo Jewish Review*
Cape Town, So. Africa....*The South African Jewish Chronicle*
Cherry Hill, N. J.....*The Voice*
Chicago, Ill.......*The Sentinel*
Cincinnati, Ohio..*Every Friday*
Columbus, Ohio....*Ohio Jewish Chronicle*
Denver, Colo..*The Jewish News*
Des Moines, Iowa....*The News Letter*
Detroit, Mich....*Detroit Jewish News*
Douglaston, N. Y....*The Scroll*
East St. Louis, Ill......*Jewish Community News*
El Paso, Texas.........*Jewish Community Voice*
Fresno, Cal.....*Central Valley Jewish Heritage*
Glasgow, Scotland..*The Jewish Echo*
Indianapolis, Ind...*The Indiana Jewish Chronicle*
Jacksonville, Fla. ....*Southern Jewish Weekly*
Jericho, L. I., N.Y.......*Shofar*
Jersey City, N. J...*The Jewish Standard*
Johannesburg, So. Africa......*Zionist Record*
Kansas City, Mo.......*Jewish Chronicle*
Long Island, N. Y.....*The Long Island Jewish Press*
Los Angeles, Calif...*The Jewish Voice*
Manchester, Eng.......*Jewish Telegraph*
Melbourne, Australia....*Jewish Herald*
Memphis, Tenn.........*Hebrew Watchman*
Miami, Fla.........*The Jewish Floridian*
Minneapolis, Minn.........*The American Jewish World*

Montreal, Canada.......*Jewish Chronicle*
Nashville, Tenn...*The Observer*
Newark, N. J........*American Jewish Ledger*
New York, N. Y.....*American Examiner*
New York, N. Y....*World Over*
New York, N. Y........*Young Judaean*
Philadelphia, Pa........*Jewish Exponent*
Phoenix, Ariz...*Phoenix Jewish News*
Pittsburgh, Pa.........*Jewish Chronicle*
San Antonio, Tex...*B'nai B'rith Voice*
San Diego, Calif. ...*Southwest Jewish Press*
San Francisco, Calif. ..*Jewish Community Bulletin*
Scranton, Pa........*The Argus*
South Bend, Ind..........*Our Community*
Springfield, Mass.......*Jewish Weekly News*
St. Louis, Mo.....*Jewish Light*
St. Paul, Minn.......*St. Paul Jewish News*
Sydney, Australia......*Jewish Times*
Sydney, Australia.*Jewish News*
Toronto, Canada.....*The Daily Hebrew Journal*
Tucson, Ariz.......*The Arizona Post*
Utica, N. Y...........*Jewish Community News*
Vancouver, Canada ....*Jewish Western Bulletin*
Washington, D. C...*The Jewish Digest*
Washington, D. C....*The B'nai B'rith Women's World*
Washington, D. C.........*The National Jewish Monthly*
Winnipeg, Canada..*The Jewish Post*

"That's Jack, the president of our congregation.
He's always been a middle-of-the-roader."

"James, if the rabbi says it's trefe, give him an argument."

**"If only the others sold like that
Talmudic Judaism!"**

"Now don't forget, Davey, move your lips when
I start the Bar-Mitzvah record."

"Boy, these Bar Mitzvahs are real killers!"

"And you, my dear, should also meet a good-looking Jewish man and keep a good Jewish home and raise a good Jewish boy who should become a good Jewish doctor."

"Gentlemen, it's to be an Orthodox shul, so please—no pig iron."

"Mama! Come quick . . . *er redt yiddish!*"

"Please, Doctor, not with a milchidicke knife!"

"And tomorrow, we'll have Orthodox Sabbath services for our delegates from 9 to 12 o'clock, Conservative services from 10 to 12, and Reform services from 10:30 to 11."

"And I want you children to always remember—
he's still your father, a schlemiel and a nudnik
though he may be!"

"My son, the analyst!"

"It hurts on the Lower East Side."

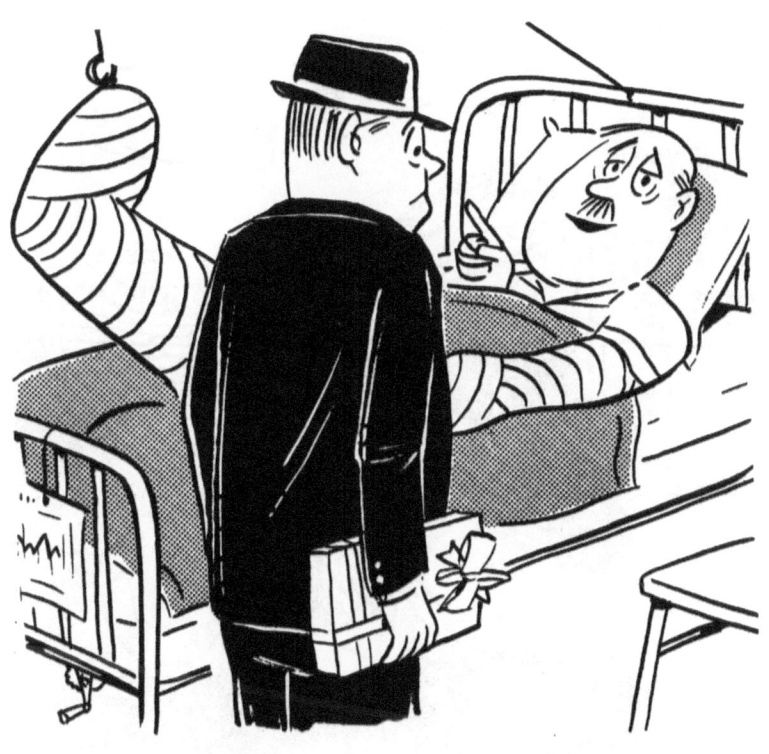

"And, Sam, to help me forget my small troubles
. . . God, in His infinite wisdom, gave me a major
affliction."

"We're retiring the old one."

"It's our first self-davening prayer book . . .
comes complete with transistor batteries."

"To the Galicianer Shul, please!"

"And the next question for discussion is: ' "Can the Toupee Be Considered a Yarmalke Substitute?' "

"And for Brotherhood Week, we're serving
matzo balls in our minestrone soup."

"But the doctor told me to take them three times
a day, *religiously!*"

"I don't care if it has been sterilized, it still isn't Kosher L'Pesach!"

"And first I will give you the Traditional version."

"After trying liquid hydrogen, solid propellants, and what not . . . we finally used horseradish."

"Listen to him! With my people suffering 3,000
years of persecution and misery, he wants
I should be emotionally secure."

"The artist calls it 'The Jew in a Gentile World.' "

"You got me all wrong, Sam. It's not that I want
to join . . . it's that I want the RIGHT to REFUSE!"

"Gentlemen, it's true now there are only two
Jews in our 78 plants, but by next year—and
with bold and courageous action on our part
—we intend to DOUBLE that number."

"Manny! What a spot for a gambling casino!"

When the Messiah Comes...

"No, Bob, contrary to what you said, I insist that Rabbi Eleazer ben Arach demonstrated much greater sagacity and acumen in Talmudic discourse than his contemporary, Rabbi Joshua ben Hananiah."

"Ah, Molly, if we Jews could only have
something as lovely as that 23rd Psalm!"

"Morris, go over and reason with them. Show
them how bigotry is irrational."

"Ah, Max, that's what I love about a full meal in a Jewish restaurant. Before you begin—you're FULL!"

"They had to set 'em up this way . . . no one wanted to sit on the extreme right or left."

"Then, gentlemen, it's agreed that our new rabbi should be a man with strong opinions, and with the strength not to express them."

"And then that bonnie lad, Judah McCabee, came and freed the Jews from . . ."

"And though homiletically sound, I found Rabbi Nubkin's sermon contained too much exegesis without sufficient expatiation on his primary text."

"Thank goodness! Now if they don't show up at services tonight, at least I have a good excuse."

"Sam always wanted to be buried in the soil of Israel."

"And we've named him Duncan Mason from Pittsburgh . . . after his grandfather, Dovid Meyer from Pinsk."

"Here's an odd one, Rabbi, . . . a couple for
marriage, and they're both Jewish!"

"And because of the lack of time, we'll defer our
discussion on 'The Extreme Right and Its Imminent
Threat to Jewish Survival' . . . till next year's convention in Miami."

"I'm sorry, Rabbi Nubkin, I can't come to services tonight. It's the only time we could find for our temple-board meeting."

"What a gossiper that Mrs. Shapiro is! She repeats everything I say about the rabbi's wife."

"Our cantor? The greatest! He gives you 4,000
years of Jewish suffering with one kvetch."

"Morris gets real enthused now that we've discovered this new No-Cal wine for Kiddush!"

"The front rows are reserved for the pious and
the humble."

"Why, Zede—we'd never think of a Christmas
tree without a Star of David on top!"

"Let's close up now, Morris, it's time for Mincha."

"I just can't understand how my son does so well in Hebrew school when's he's such a poor student in public school."

"Two plus two—God willing—makes four."

"But, Bobe, all I wanted was a glass of water!"

"Oh, now I see . . . you diaper him like a
hamantaschen!"

"If we include the cantor, the shammas, and the
organist . . . we've almost got a 'Minyan
in Residence'!"

"My God! He's been locked in here since last Yom Kippur!"

"And, Sam, if you want it to be a 'Festival of Freedom' for me, too . . . next year we go to the Community Seder at the temple."

"I still prefer the cave . . . a succah is not
a house!"

"Sleep, my child, sleep . . . and some day you will grow up to know Torah, good deeds, and electronic engineering."

"And, Pop, . . . if I fulfill all the 613 mitzvoth,
could I someday also become president of
the shul?"

"Sam, have 'em JOIN you in the Hebrew bless-
inq over the bread . . . then they'll never know
you forgot the words."

"I guess it's because there are so many Cohens!"

"Purim is called the 'Feast of Lots' . . . because on
this day we all eat LOTS of hamantaschen!"

"All right. Who's the wise guy that put the
bubble bath in the mikvah?"

"My philosophy of life? It's very simple, Max.
Whatever is . . . *is wrong!*"

"Now, Sam, that's what I call RELIGION!"

"And it shall come to pass in the end of days,
O Daughters of Moab, that among all of the
animals of the field, thou shalt choose the
lowly mink."

GLOSSARY

*For readers unfamiliar with Jewish terms
and Yiddish words, the following
definitions are presented . . .*

BAR MITZVAH: Name for confirmed Jewish boy, thirteen years old; or name of ceremony itself.

BOBE: Grandmother.

CHANUKAH: Eight-day festival celebrated in December in honor of ancient Jewish struggle for religious freedom.

CHASANAH: Wedding.

DAVENING: Praying.

ER REDT YIDDISH: "He speaks Yiddish."

GELT: Money.

HAMANTASCHEN: Triangular-shaped pastry eaten on the Jewish Festival of Purim.

KIDDUSH: Blessing over a cup of wine consecrating the Sabbath or a holiday.

KOSHER: Conforming with Jewish dietary laws.

KOSHER L'PESACH: Conforming with Jewish dietary laws pertaining to Passover.

KVETCH: To whine or complain; here used as a sigh of suffering.

MAZEL-TOV: Good luck.

MIKVAH: Indoor bath used for Jewish ritual purposes.

MILCHIDICKE: Pertaining to dairy foods for which there are exclusive utensils in Jewish ritual regulations.

MINCHA: Afternoon service of the Jewish liturgy.

MINYAN: A minimum congregation of ten men.

MITZVOTH: Biblical or Rabbinic commandments.

NUDNIK: A bore.

SEDER: Religious home service dealing with the Exodus; celebrated on the first two nights of Passover.

SHAMMAS: A Jewish sexton.

SHLEMIEL: A clumsy, inept person.

SHOKELS: Rocks back and forth.

SHUL: Synagogue.

SUCCAH: A thatched-roof booth.

TALLIS: Prayer shawl.

TREFE: Food forbidden by dietary laws.

YARMALKE: Skullcap worn in the synagogue.

YOM KIPPUR: The Day of Atonement.

ZEDE: Grandfather.

BAGEL POWER

PUBLISHER'S NOTE

BAGEL POWER is a treasury of Jewish cartoon fun, demonstrating what happens as an old, traditional way of life meets head-on with a mechanized, modern society. In fine salty style, these delightful spoofs on real contemporary problems touch on universal experience time and time again.

Dayenu (Da-yay-noo) cartoons are the creation of a two-man team. Rabbi Henry Rabin is Executive Director of Los Angeles Hillel Council; he is the idea man. Artist Leonard Pritikin draws the cartoons when he isn't busy with his Southern California advertising-marketing firm. Together they are "Henry Leonard," and their cartoons have appeared in over 60 Anglo-Jewish publications for over a decade.

We think these cartoons deserve a wider audience. As you turn these pages, we know that you will agree.

GLOSSARY

For readers unfamiliar with Jewish terms
and Yiddish words, the following
definitions are presented....

BAR MITZVAH: Name for confirmed Jewish boy, thirteen
years old; or name of ceremony itself.
BOBE: Grandmother.
CHALEH: A braided loaf of white bread, glazed with egg
white.
DAVENING: Praying.
KOSHER: Conforming with Jewish dietary laws.
MATZOS: Unleavened bread.
MINYAN: A religious congregation of at least ten men.
ROSH HASHONAH: Jewish New Year.
SHABBAS: Sabbath or Saturday.
SHADCHAN: Marriage broker.
SHOFAR: A ram's horn that is blown in synagogue during
the High Holidays.
SHUL: Synagogue.
SIDDUR: The daily and Sabbath prayer book.
SUCCAH: A thatched-roof booth.
TALMUD: The basic body of Jewish Oral Law.
YOM KIPPUR: The Day of Atonement.

"It's good you're watching, Epstein...
but it would be better if you came to shul
once in a while."

"We've distributed 1500 Yom Kippur tickets for the 1000 seats in our temple. Gentlemen, let us now pray for atonement...and for *rain* on Yom Kippur night!"

"I'm joining, Rabbi, 'cause I only want to date
Jewish boys, observe the Jewish customs,
and learn the Talmud."

"And this testimonial goes to Mr. Epstein...the Anonymous-Donor-of-the-Year."

"And when they said he couldn't be president...
Bernie went into business for himself."

WHY RABBIS GET GREY AT THE TEMPLES:

"Why can't you perform my son's wedding on Shabbas? After all, the girl he's going to marry isn't Jewish!"

WHY RABBIS GET GREY AT THE TEMPLES:

**"How dare you assign my son a Bar Mitzvah
date that is so inconvenient for my caterer!"**

"Our poor Rabbi...he's got to work on *Shabbas!*"

A social evening with Rabbi Nubkin.

"And tonight, instead of a speech, I'm going to
say something."

"Goot Shabbas, Mr. Pinsker...and which shul
didn't you go to this morning?"

"Sure I'm still a non-believer, but just in case I'm wrong...pass the *Siddur!*"

"And when the bulbs flash on...then it's time
for you to say 'Amen.'"

WHY RABBIS GET GREY AT THE TEMPLES:

"Darling, at the Bar Mitzvah today, take it easy on the schnapps and chopped liver... and in your sermon, take it easy on the congregation."

"And you can imagine what it's going to do to the
congregation!"

"Gentlemen, I'm ready to serve my people in any capacity whatsoever...as long as I am *chairman*."

**"And since you're kosher, Rabbi...for you we've
prepared a *special* shrimp salad!"**

"Molly's at the wheel tonight...I never drive on Shabbas!"

"Molly, the difference between you and me is
fundamental. You say the bottle is half empty—
I say it's half full."

"And when your Ma and I argue, Haskele—never interfere. It's the only pleasure we still have left!"

"With so many *vice* presidents, they must be awfully wicked!"

"Rabbi, the Temple Board, by majority of 14 to 12,
voted you a speedy recovery."

"And this year's winner of the
International Purim Queen Esther Contest is
Miss Aban Abdul of Egypt!"

**"My fortune cookie message reads:
'Give to the United Jewish Fund'!"**

"And every Yom Kippur I always skip one meal....
It makes me feel more Jewish."

"And how about some of you 'cats' coming to services tonight . . . we're having a *Pray-In!*"

"Learn, baby, learn!"

"Why don't you call it, 'How I won the Six Day
War from My Suite in the Tel Aviv Hilton'...?"

"And when you return to New York, give my best
regards to my cousins, the Cohens.
They live somewhere in Flatbush."

"My Maxie is now so assimilated, he takes his
Shabbas nap on Sunday!"

"Shabbas in Slabotke was never like this!"

"And my fifth question is, 'When do we eat?'"

**"And with our new automatic pilot, you can use
the captain for a minyan."**

"Send us two more of each.... We're expecting a
lot of American tourists this month!"

"And as my Bobe used to say, 'If you stop fighting... you'll have peace!'"

"My mom's got me so brainwashed...
I've decided to marry a Jewish girl."

"Sam sure uses the latest methods!"

"Then it is agreed that above all else...our new Rabbi should play golf in the low 70's!"

"Daddy, did God create them, too?"

**"What you say about me, Molly, hurts so much...
it must be true. Thank you ever so much for your
criticism!"**

"It fell with his second blast!"

"Morris hid the matzoh so well, he can't find it himself!"

"Pop, why do they hide the choir?
Are they ashamed of them?"

**"Turn-away crowds every Shabbas...
since we hired that guru!"**

"I don't hear you davening, David."

"Egg-Twist?—Oh, you mean a *chaleh!*"

"And my mom says that when I grow up, I can
marry anyone I want, as long as she's a nice
Jewish girl from a kosher, respectable,
upper-middle-class home."

"First eat, eat, my child—then we'll talk."

"And above all, you must learn to take *bold* positions with which *no one* will disagree!"

"The succah itself is reasonable. It's those darn
extras, like heater, tinted-glass windows, and
hi-fi stereo, that add up."

"Built 'em both myself—but that's the shul I don't go to."

"And to think that only last year he painted them for Jewish delicatessens!"

"And in our economy package—you get the temple
at 2 P.M., and the *Junior* Rabbi."

His mother was an Hungarian Jew.
His father, African-American.
Ollie Harrington became the greatest
cartoonist in the Black newspapers of
the twentieth century.

Published by **About Comics**.
Publishing things that oughta be published.